Maurice Sendak's Seven Little Monsters

Monsters in Space

Story by ARTHUR YORINKS

Pictures by RAYMOND JAFELICE

VOLO
Hyperion Books for Children

For Lynn Caponera
—A.Y.

To Maurice and my own eight little monsters,
Gwendolynne, James, Roberta, Alexander, Peter,
Elizabeth, Samantha, and Aidan.
—R.J.

Seven Little Monsters characters © 1975, 1977 Maurice Sendak
All other material © 2003 Hyperion Books for Children
Volo® is a registered trademark of Disney Enterprises, Inc.
The Volo colophon is a trademark of Disney Enterprises, Inc.

Printed in the United States of America
First Edition
1 3 5 7 9 10 8 6 4 2

This book is set in 18-point Minion.

ISBN 0-7868-1775-5

Visit www.volobooks.com

One Saturday, after it had stopped raining, the seven little monsters decided to visit Pluto in outer space.

So they took some boxes, an empty family-size can of beans, a small ladder, some dials they'd been saving, a clothes hanger, their toothbrushes, a map, a few cans of tuna fish, a little mayonnaise, some rye bread, and a pack of gum, and built a spaceship and blasted off.

"This is Captain Seven," said Seven. "The first planet we see should be Neptune."

"I see it!" said Five.

"Can't I drive?" asked Three.

"We all have our jobs," said Captain Seven.

"You're the lookout!"

"But what do I do?" asked Three.

"You look out the window!" answered Seven.

"What about me?" said One.
"Why do I always have to be the wings?"
"You're a natural," said Four.

They passed a few more planets, and
some comets went whizzing by. Suddenly,
Three pointed out the window. "I'm looking
out and I see something!" he shouted.
"It's Pluto!" cried Six.

Captain Seven spun into action. "Two," he commanded, "what's the temperature outside?"

Two stuck his nose out the window and said, "It's cold."

"Okay, everyone put on your spacesuits and prepare for landing," Seven said.

The seven little monsters got into their spacesuits and strapped themselves in as their spaceship headed straight toward Pluto.

"Five—the brakes!" commanded Captain Seven. Five applied the brakes with his feet and both hands, and the ship came to a sudden stop. The monsters carefully climbed outside.

"I'm looking, I'm looking," said Three.
"But I don't see anything."

"Figures," said Four. "All this way for nothing. Let's eat." The seven monsters made a little picnic.

"I'm looking again," said Three, "and I see something, Captain . . . uh-oh!" Some kind of creature from Pluto was heading straight for them. Captain Seven sprang into action.

"Six," he said, "go see who it is."

Six straightened her tutu, walked toward
the alien, and raised her hand. "We come in
peace. Take us to your leader!" she said.

"I *am* the leader!" said the alien. "I am Pluto, of the planet Pluto."

"But you're just a dog!" said Six. Just as she said that, Pluto gave out a howl—and before she knew it, a whole pack of dogs had come from everywhere.

"Captain," said Six. "We have a problem."
All the monsters stood behind their captain.

"I am Seven, from Earth," said Seven. "We offer—" and before he could say another word, Pluto cried, "Tuna sandwiches!" And all the aliens from Pluto pounced on the sandwiches and ate them like there was no tomorrow.

The seven little monsters ran for their ship,
closed the hatch, and quickly blasted off.

"That was a close one," said Three.
"You said it," Five said.

"I'm starving," said Four.

"Calling Mama." Captain got on the space
phone and called. "Calling Mama. We're hungry!
Do you read me?"

"This is Mama," said Mama. "I read you clear and loud. Come, my little pudding heads, come and have a little chicken soup, and there's roast beef and potatoes, and even chocolate pudding."

The seven little monsters couldn't get back
to Earth quick enough.

And they ate their dinner.